Little Red Robin

The Purple
Butterfly

Do you have all the Little Red Robin books?

☐ Buster's Big Surprise
☐ The Purple Butterfly
☐ How Bobby Got His Pet
☐ We are Super!
☐ New Friends
☐ Robo-Robbie

Also available as ebooks

If you feel ready to read a longer book,
look out for more stories about Magic Molly

The Purple Butterfly

Little Red
Robin

Holly Webb

Illustrated by Erica Jane Waters

SCHOLASTIC

Scholastic Children's Books
An imprint of Scholastic Ltd.
Euston House, 24 Eversholt Street
London, NW1 1DB, UK
Registered office: Westfield Road, Southam, Warwickshire, CV47 0RA
SCHOLASTIC and associated logos are trademarks and/or registered
trademarks of Scholastic Inc.

First published in the UK in 2014 by Scholastic Ltd

ISBN 978 1407 13882 4

A CIP catalogue record for this book is available from the British Library

Printed in China.

1 3 5 7 9 10 8 6 4 2

www.scholastic.co.uk/zone

Molly looked hopefully at the back door, which
led out into the yard. Just across the yard was her
dad's surgery.

Molly's dad was a vet, and his surgery was one of her favourite places in the whole world. Molly loved animals, and there were always interesting new pets at the surgery.

Molly was hoping to see Fred. He was a gorgeous lop-eared rabbit, and he was staying at the surgery while his owners were on holiday.

Fred was so
friendly! Molly
had even hidden
a carrot in the
pocket of her
shorts, to feed
him with.

"Were you looking for Dad, Molly?" said Mum.
"He's really busy this afternoon. Why don't you
go and practise your skipping again? Or you and
Kitty could help me make cupcakes."

"Cake!" Molly's little sister Kitty wriggled out from under the kitchen table. She was covered in streaks of felt tip pen – she looked like she'd been drawing on herself, instead of her big pad of paper.

It was too hot for cooking, Molly thought. "I'll come back and help you ice the cakes," she told Mum. "I just feel like being outside for a bit."

Molly hoped that Dad might let her take Fred the rabbit out into the garden. The grass was full of dandelions. Mum kept trying to dig them up, but Molly thought that it would be a much better idea to feed them to a hungry rabbit.

There were huge, delicious-looking dandelions
dotted all over the garden, just opening their
bright yellow sunshiny flowers. Molly thought
that perhaps she could pick some and give them
to Dad later? If she kept them in water, they'd
be a nice treat for Fred, even if he wasn't allowed
to go out and find them for himself.

Molly took off her shoes and began to collect
a great big bunch of dandelions. She liked the
feeling of the long, cool grass all round her feet.
She picked some dandelion leaves too. The new,
shiny green ones looked juicy and delicious – for a
rabbit, anyway.

The clouds had blown away now, and the sun was blazing down. Molly scurried around, picking the fat yellow dandelions, until she had a huge handful.

It was so sunny, she filled up Kitty's toy bucket with water, to keep the flowers fresh.

When she had picked a big bunch, Molly lay down on her front in the long grass. She cupped her chin in her hands and stared down in between the grass stems. She knew if she watched for long enough she'd see an ant, or a little beetle. They always looked so busy.

Molly loved to imagine where they were going and what they were thinking about as they hurried through the huge forests of grass.

Molly yawned. The sun was so lovely and warm on her hair and her bare feet. A long line of ants was marching through the grass under her nose. Molly giggled. She could imagine them singing a marching song as they strode along.

Suddenly, out of the corner of her eye, Molly saw a flash of colour. She looked up in surprise. Perhaps Kitty had come out into the garden? But no, it wasn't Kitty.

A gorgeous, velvety purple butterfly was perched on a nearby grass stem. It fluttered its wings up and down, and Molly laughed in delight. She had never seen such a lovely colour.

The butterfly twitched its feelers, then turned towards Molly a little, gently flapping its wings. Molly couldn't help thinking that it was trying to get her attention.

The underneath of its wings were a soft purple-blue, with beautiful dots and stripes. As the butterfly opened and closed its wings, the colours seemed to ripple and glow.

The butterfly's body was covered in soft black fur. Molly longed to stroke it, but she didn't reach out to touch. The butterfly was so perfect and delicate, Molly thought she might hurt it.

"You can touch if you like. . ." said a tiny voice, like the ringing of little bells.

Molly blinked. She must have imagined the voice. Butterflies didn't talk, did they?

"Didn't you hear me?" said the silvery voice.
"Wouldn't you like to stroke my fur? It's very soft."
"Me. . .?" Molly whispered, looking around.

"Yes, of course you! We're the only ones here! Except for those ants, and they wouldn't want to. Ants are very boring things."

"Are they?" Molly gulped. She was talking to a butterfly. She reached out one careful finger and ran it down the dark fur. It was amazingly soft.

"Very nice." The butterfly twitched its wings.
"Could you rub a little further down? I've got a
bit of an itch there. Ooooh, that's it. Perfect.

"What were we talking about? Oh, yes, ants. Mmmm. Ants are all work, work, work. They don't ever stop to chat. Of course, they wouldn't have much to talk about, poor things. No wings, you see. They don't fly. So nothing interesting ever happens to them."

"I can't fly either," Molly pointed out, rather sadly.

"Can't you?" The butterfly sounded quite shocked. "Really? And look at the size of you! Surely you could have found the time to grow some wings?"

"I don't think humans work like that. I can run."

"Hmmm. Show me," the butterfly demanded.
Molly jumped up, and ran down the garden as
fast as she could.

The purple butterfly
fluttered after her,
twirling and swooping,
keeping up with her
easily. Molly stopped
to lean on the side of
the garden shed. She
was out of breath.

"Yes, I see," said the butterfly. "Quite nice, I suppose. But it's nothing compared to flying. Wouldn't you like to try?"

"Of course!" Molly glared at the butterfly. "But I told you, I can't!"

"Nonsense. Come a little closer." The butterfly fluttered along the shed window sill closer to Molly. "Right up close to me. That's it."

Molly stared – it was the closest she had ever been to a butterfly, and she could see every detail. Even its eyes! They were round, and glittery yellow, and rather bossy-looking. The butterfly nodded at her importantly.

It began to flap its purple-blue wings back and forth very fast – so fast that they blurred into a sparkling purplish mist.

Molly gasped. The misty colour was rising up off the butterfly's wings now, filling the air with shimmering blue. "What's happening?" she cried.

"Magic spell!" the butterfly squeaked. "Can't talk now!"

Molly shivered as the purple-blue magic wrapped
itself around her, and the back of her neck tickled.
She giggled and twitched – and an
enormous pair of purple
wings burst out of
the back of her
pink T-shirt.

"There!" the butterfly said triumphantly. "You look an awful lot nicer now, don't you think?"

Molly peered over her shoulder, gazing at the velvet-soft wings fluttering behind her. She gave them a tiny flap, just to try them out, and felt her toes lift off the ground. "Oh! I can fly!"

The butterfly made an impatient sort of snorting noise. "Well, of course! What do you think I gave you wings for? Come on!"

And with that, the butterfly fluttered off into the air, with the sun glinting on its brilliant purple wings. "Flap! Flap hard!"

Molly twitched the wings again, wishing and
wishing. Please, please, please…

She was up! She was in the air! Molly squealed
and swooped, diving down to skim the grass, and
then up, as far as the top of the tall oak tree at
the end of the garden. Her house looked tiny
from up here!

"Better than running, isn't it?" the butterfly called, twirling round and round her.

"Oh yes!" Molly cried back. "It's better than anything!" She swooped right over the top of the tree, giggling as she saw a shocked-looking squirrel dive back into a hole in the trunk.

"Molly! Molly! Butterflies!" called a voice
from below.

Molly fluttered back around the oak tree.
"That's my little sister calling," she told the
butterfly. "I ought to go back – they'll be wondering
where I am."

The butterfly twitched its feelers. "Yes, and the spell won't last much longer. You should probably make sure you land before those wings disappear."

Molly gulped. She really was ever such a long way up. She fluttered the beautiful wings gently, swooping down to land with a gentle bump on the grass. Then she let out a little sigh of relief.

Flying was wonderful, but the grass felt comforting and firm under her toes. The wings had gone, she realized suddenly.

"Goodbye!" the butterfly called, twirling up into the sky again. "Come flying again soon!"

"Molly, did you see that beautiful butterfly?" her mum asked, hurrying down the garden towards her. "It looked like a Purple Emperor. I've never seen one here before."

Molly nodded, and blinked. She could just see the purple butterfly, darting away past the oak tree. She wriggled her shoulders, and they felt just like they always did. Had it all been a dream? Perhaps she had just fallen asleep in the sunshine, and only dreamed that she was flying?

"There were two. . ." Kitty was staring up into the sky, frowning. "A little one, and a big one. . . With big wings. And a pink top. . ." She looked back at Molly, her eyes very wide, and Molly put her finger to her lips, smiling.

"Ssshhhh," she whispered to her little sister. "It's a secret! Maybe next time, you can come too. . ."